Yoo hoo, Mr Crab!

For more information about my books, please go to my website:
https://booksbyjennywatt.com

Yoo hoo, Mr Crab!

Written by Jenny Watt

Illustrated by Christine Cagara
(Email: *cagara.christine18@gmail.com*)

ISBN 978-1-915128-10-2

For Tom

Mr Crab was a solitary fellow.
He lived in a cozy hole he had dug for himself.
Every morning, he woke up early and stretched
his legs on the beach.

When the weather was good, he swam out to the Big Rock in the Sea.

In the evenings, he listened to the sound of the waves as the sun set.

Day after day, Mr Crab enjoyed his quiet life. Until one morning, as he was climbing out of his hole, he heard someone call...

Who could it be, so early in the morning?
A pretty blue crab scuttled towards him, waving
a pink scarf.

"Hello Mr Crab!" she said.
"I'm SO glad to find you up already."
Mr. Crab looked at her with his big eyes.

"My name is Lucy. I've come to invite you to tomorrow's Crab Picnic. It starts at 4 o'clock. Everyone will be there!"

Mr Crab thought, "A picnic! With other crabs!"
Mr Crab was not happy. He *liked* being alone.
But before he could say anything, Lucy smiled
and said, "I hope you will come!"
And off she went.

Mr Crab worried about the picnic all day.
He could just stay at home tomorrow.
But what if Lucy came to look for him?

So early the next morning, instead of going to the picnic, Mr Crab packed his bag and carried it down the beach until he came to another spot.

There he began to dig, and by the time the sun had risen in the sky, he had made a new home. "It has a nice view," thought Mr Crab, and began to relax. But the next morning, he heard Lucy call...

Lucy scuttled up to him.
"Oh Mr Crab, I see that you've moved," said Lucy.
"We were sorry to miss you at the picnic.
It was such a success that we've decided to
have another one!"

"Perhaps next time we'll have it here!" said Lucy.
Mr Crab was horrified.
The whole town, coming to his home!

So, Mr Crab packed his bag again
and moved even further down the beach.
But the next day, even before he had climbed out
of his hole, he heard Lucy call...

This time, she invited him for tea in town.

So Mr Crab moved again...
And again...
But every time he thought he was safe,
he heard Lucy call...

By the time he had dug his twentieth home,
Mr Crab was tired of moving.

"I can't keep digging new holes," he said to himself.
Then he had a brilliant idea.
"I'll move to the Big Rock in the Sea! Lucy won't
be able to follow me there."

So Mr Crab packed his bag and made his way towards his old home. As he got closer, he was surprised to see lots of other crabs. "That's funny," he thought. "I don't remember having any neighbours."
Just then, he heard Lucy call ...

And who should crawl out of his old home, but Lucy!

Mr Crab dropped his bag in surprise and sputtered, "What are you doing here?"

Lucy smiled. "After you moved, I thought it would be a pity to leave such a fine hole empty. But if you want to move back, I can always move next door."

"Next door?" asked Mr Crab.

"Yes, my brother Jimmy lives next door, and my Aunt Suzy lives over there, and, well, most of my family lives here now. And it's all thanks to you!"

"Thanks to me?" said Mr Crab.

"Why of course! It was YOU who built this town!"

Mr Crab was astonished.
As he looked around, he realised that these were the holes he had dug for himself!
They stretched along the beach, as far as his eyes could see.

"Please stay for tea, Mr Crab," said Lucy.
Mr Crab looked at the sea. It was too late to swim
to the Big Rock. He looked back towards his home.
It was a long walk away.

So Mr Crab finally took a cup of tea from Lucy. And as he sipped his tea, he felt a funny feeling. It was rather nice to drink tea with another crab!

So the next morning, he came back and had another cup with Lucy.
And the next day.
And the next.

And together, they listened to the sound of the waves as the sun set.

The End

Printed in Great Britain
by Amazon

38551040R00021